DARK IS

& OTHER WYRD TALES

SUSAN EARLAM

SPELEOREX PRESS

Dark Is The Water by Susan Earlam

https://susanearlam.com

Copyright © 2022 by Susan Earlam / Speleorex Press

Cover by Ana Milani- Instagram @omnifantasmicdraws

Ebook ISBN: 978-1-8383794-4-5
Paperback ISBN: 978-1-8383794-3-8

—·—

CONTENTS

1

BABY

The shower was still bloody. They hadn't cleaned it. She couldn't stand to look at it every day whilst the baby lay in intensive care. This was their room, a private room, she wanted to be proud of it. She asked the nurse for something to clean it with.

She scrubbed the shower floor and the tiles on either side. The water made the blood come back to life. Pinky red rivulets streamed down into the plug. She didn't know if it was hers or the baby's.

They stayed together a while after the birth. Then tests showed the baby needed surgery.

She scrubbed harder and wondered how could they operate on something so small, so fragile. It was the baby's heart, they'd said. It needed replacing. There were three varieties available; squirrel, monkey or cat. She chose cat of course. Anything to bring the baby closer to the family. The surgeon had explained that his work was at the forefront of medicine. In a few years, this would be normal. She was lucky to have come into this particular hospital during labour.

The water wasn't going down quick enough. Something was blocking its way in the plug. She switched the shower off and fished around the opening. Hair, tissue, clots of blood. She pulled it all out and lay it on a towel on the floor. The pink water remained. She called the nurse; they said they'd sort it. She didn't believe them.

But someone did come this time. A caretaker, an odd-job man. She wrapped herself tighter in her bathrobe as he poked around the plughole with something that looked like a long mascara wand.

'There is something here alright,' he said.

'No shit,' she whispered to herself.

There was a guttural belch from the plug and a sound of victory from the handyman.

'It's only a bloody furball,' he said. 'Have you got a cat?'

He lay the long, hairy sausage beside the other artefacts on the towel. She was left in pieces all over again.

2

THE FIELD

T he merging of the community was essential. Fate, some said; others stayed quiet. The festival occurred on a blue moon. The families in the village calculated the dates years in advance and made a note of them in their diaries. Dependant on the skies, the festival was every two to three years. It was such an important occasion for the community that many youths already had their sights set on it as a place to meet their mate, a future breeding situation. More than half the couples in the town had met this way. This gave these people a pass.

Paired couples always looked so smug at the festival. It put a lot of pressure on Matilda as one of the lucky couples were her parents. Elevated into town society like deities. The elders who'd been together the longest would roll into the cricket ground on floats. Matilda could barely recall the last festival, so much had happened, but she saw the evidence of each one on the hall stairway of the house she shared

with her parents. Photographs, some in black and white.
Mum looking beautiful and Dad handsome; both getting
older in each shot. In one of them, Matilda peeps around
her mum's white calico dress, hot pink pansies pinned into
her hair. She doesn't remember it.

At school, there's been talk of little else.

"Who is your first choice? Who is your second?" It was all
you could hear on entering the girl's toilets. The main issue
concerning them was the lack of boys. There weren't many
of the right age within the population of the town. Many
had been absent in the month leading up to the festival.
Parents wanting to protect their sons, scared of what a
young girl might do; knowing how much power they
wielded, knowing their boys were weak-willed and riddled
with hormones, easily seduced, easily led. Although that
wasn't Matilda's problem; she didn't like boys, she was
already in love with her best friend, Sarah. Sarah was the
most magical creature Matilda had ever seen. She was
everything a boy wasn't, soft, beautiful, kind. Matilda knew
her mother suspected something.

"The Blue Moon Festival will see you right, it sees
everyone right. You're of age now."

The family of three prepared themselves. Matilda's father
pulled out a gown made for Matilda. Calico pleats fell from
her collarbone and dropped to her feet. The fibres itched
her skin. Her parents retrieved the festival trunk from the
loft and pulled out their unwashed gowns. Smudges of
grass, splashes of red wine, and mud caked on the hem.
Once someone met their partner, they had to attend each

festival wearing the same gown. That way, the coupling was recognised. That way, they were safe. Matilda's mother braided her hair and piled it onto her daughter's head, as was tradition. Then she did her own. Her father brushed his hair and sprayed it with water to hold it in place. They all wore boots, as the grass would be muddy.

Her parents left their house first. They had to gather with the other elders and get on the floats before their grand entrance. Matilda sat in front of her bedroom mirror and applied lipstick. Her eyes were watery. What to do? Sarah would be there, of course. Could they not just choose each other? Matilda still wasn't sure that Sarah's feelings would translate into action. They didn't seem as strong as her own, as vivid.

It was dusk and the chill in the air marking the start of autumn brushed Matilda's skin, wrapping itself like a cold ribbon around her neck. She closed the gate that marked the border between the street and her home. The sound of music floated up from the cricket ground. She wanted to run. Leave. Only thoughts of Sarah stopped the idea.

Her parents lived high in the village, in direct relation to their high and lengthy position within the community. The lane curved downwards like a snake toward the unlit cricket ground. The night fell, the lanterns in the front gardens led the way. Matilda joined the throng of villagers, making their way into the wide field that doubled as the cricket ground in summer. It had a large, shallow drum in the centre, wheeled in earlier, no doubt by her father and his friends. She vaguely remembered helping him one year with it.

They had loaded the drum with wood and firelighters and a pig was impaled from a spit at one side. There was rain in the air and they couldn't risk the fire not starting. She looked around for someone to stand with, Sarah or a boy from school, but couldn't see anyone recognisable. Instead, the faces in the crowd stared at her with greyed out eyes, the features fuzzy because of the gloom. The cold dug further into her neck and the music halted.

It was time for the floats. The small crowd parted and in purred the local milk float. It too was dressed in a costume of white, billowing fabric; like a valance around a bed, hiding the mess underneath. It held the symbol of the festival a large sphere of blue, representing the moon. On the second float stood Matilda's parents. She locked eyes with her mother as they drove past. Her father looked out the opposite way. There was no smile of recognition, no conspiratorial wink. The throne sat between them as they stood on the back of the float. Matilda noticed her mother was clinging to the back of it.

Even though the memories of previous festivals were blurry, the chair her mother was holding onto was a vivid recollection. The ivory gleamed in the moonlight; the shafts of bone held together with wires threaded through the holes drilled into bulbous heads of cartilage. It was these knobbly parts where the traditional markings were carved that her mother clung to. The bone throne seemed to glow.

Run.

RUN.

A whisper in Matilda's ear made her break eye contact with her mother and spin around, looking for the culprit. Beside her were only families with younger children, gazing in awe at the parade. It drifted past, trailers hooked onto the back of trucks, some linked together like a plastic snake from a birthday goodie bag. The last one held the mask and brought silence to the villagers. Another memory tugged at her. She couldn't pin it down. The horns on the skull seemed to reach up over the edges of the wooden trailer. Someone had attempted to cover it with a blanket.

She watched it reach the centre of the field and shook the whispers from her head. The couples climbed down from the floats and circled the drum. Someone came forward from the crowd with a lit torch and lit each of the sticks the couples held. Her father's voice rang out across the crowd. The smell of iron, of blood, filled her nostrils.

"We honour our land. We honour our home, and we are thankful. Long may our lines live."

Listen with Mother.

The whisper again.

"Let us celebrate!" The elite couples shouted as they all placed their lit torches on the fire. Within seconds, the field brightened with orange light and Matilda could look for Sarah again. Her body reacted before she registered what she saw. A cold stone grew where Matilda's heart was. Directly opposite, on the other side of the flames, Sarah was stood with a boy. They were holding hands. She'd chosen a boy. Matilda gulped back tears. Sarah hadn't seen the other girls standing behind, staring at the newly established couple. Matilda knew what was going through their minds, could almost hear the words on their lips,

"... it's not fair, why has he chosen her, I wanted him, that was her plan all along, that will be a marriage of convenience..."

The gathering seemed to exhale and relax now the fire had been lit. Matilda moved through the bodies. The wine was being passed around. Faces smiled, this time with acknowledgement. The villagers knew who her parents were, but they didn't really know her. No one did. The music started again and the pig sizzled.

The girls behind Sarah and the boy drew closer to the couple. Matilda could see one of them had her hand on his lower back, another was bold enough to curve her arm around his front. She watched as Sarah pulled him closer; the boy had a look on his face of fear mixed with elation. Matilda couldn't see Sarah's face from the angle she approached. It was excruciating.

"Hey," Matilda said as she tapped Sarah's shoulder.

Sarah spun around, manoeuvring herself underneath one of the boy's shoulders so he had his arm around her. On closer inspection, he looked dazed. There was some shiny powder by the side of his mouth.

"Where's his parents?"

"Somewhere over there, they let him go. Think they were grateful, to be honest."

"That he'd found someone? You?"

"Sorry."

The girls behind were laughing, "I think he wants a real girl," one of them said.

Matilda ignored them and lowered her voice. "We could go? Run away."

"I can't leave him. Look at them. They will rip him apart."

"Where has this loyalty come from, Sarah? What about us? What about me?"

"You'll be fine. Look who your parents are."

"It's not like that, and you know it. I heard a voice... in my head. I don't know... I need you."

"What?"

Matilda leaned in closer. Sarah's neck, so familiar. She smelt like freshly cut grass.

"I heard a whisper in my head. I think it was telling me to run."

Sarah had a look of disappointment etched across her beautiful face.

"I'm sorry it has to be this way." She sounded almost genuine, but then there was a sound of a blade being unsheathed and Matilda knew she'd been tricked. The boy Sarah had coupled with suddenly grabbed Matilda, pinning her arms to her sides. For a second the glint of metal reflected the blaze of the fire into Matilda's eyes, then the woman she loved drew the blade across her neck.

"We have her," he bellowed. Someone cheered.

Blood ran down Matilda's chest. She couldn't speak. She leaned into the boy, strangely grateful he was there and holding her up. It wasn't a deep cut, but it didn't need to be. She lost consciousness.

Matilda woke to the sound of her mother whispering in her ear as she was on her back, strapped to something hard. Above were stars and the blue moon. Her mother crouched beside her.

"I told you to run. Why didn't you run?"

Matilda couldn't reply, it was as if her mouth had gone numb.

"It's because you're the child of an elder. You're prized. You're special." She stroked Matilda's face. "It was you or all those other girls. There are thirty girls more than there are boys... And, well, we knew you didn't want to be with a boy. You wouldn't carry on the line. Those girls will."

Matilda tried to speak again, but a thickness in her mouth made it impossible. Tears formed channels from her temples to her ears.

"It's for the best." Her mother pulled away and looked at someone Matilda couldn't see. Then came her father's voice. Words of comfort spilled from his lips as they left her line of vision.

Matilda grasped at whatever was at her fingertips. She could feel wood underneath her and ropes around her limbs binding her to the relic. She was in the float trailer with the mask. One rope around her wrist was looser than the other, intentional help from her mother, perhaps? She couldn't be sure. She squeezed her hand free and lifted it to her neck. The blood there was syrupy and warm and clung to her fingertips. She reached inside her mouth, retrieved the slicked fabric and threw it to one side. The crowd were still lively, but they were some distance away.

They had used her braided hair as a hook to pin her head into place. She tugged it free and could lift her head enough to see just over the edge of the trailer where the festivities were taking place. Then her vision blurred. She could see two of everything. She lay back down and wondered how long she had left, trying to snatch at the memories that danced at the edges of her mind. What happened next? What happened last time?

Matilda reached for her other wrist and unpicked the knot, then crawled under the blanket covering the mask. In the makeshift private chamber was a smell like tar; gummy and it lingered uncomfortably at the back of her throat. Everywhere hurt. Her breath sharp in her chest. Cheeks stung as the tears fell.

The mask called to her. The sharpness of the antlers, the layers of skin and feathers, glued, stretched, cured, dried out, formed the shape of it. She lifted it and the blanket created ghost-like drapes and folds around them both. Then they became tangled and the smell of tar and blood and wet wool ran through her as she lifted it further onto her shoulders. Immediately she felt its grip around her head. Its heaviness sat and held her. It crept down her neck over the wound at her collarbone, which stung under the pressure. The mask pressed against her face, adhering itself to her cheekbones, covering her ears, pinning them back to her skull. It felt like hot soil or clay all over her head. The eye holes matched the position of her eyes, but the opening for the mouth and nose didn't align as well. She struggled for breath.

The mask continued its growth. It crept down her back and under her shoulder blades. Then it went around her front and covered her chest, sealing with itself at her neck. Her arms and legs were still free, but the mask had attached itself completely and Matilda couldn't breathe. She reached up and pulled at the face of the mask where her nose and mouth were. A strange shape formed beneath her fingers. She pulled at the mask, but it continued to grow outwards, filling her hands with a smooth, hard structure. She could breathe again. She took a gulp of the tar air and her jaw clicked when it closed. Matilda didn't need to hide anymore; she didn't need the blanket.

She pushed off the woollen fibres and felt immediately lighter. The festivities were only metres away, but she felt no threat. Her arms, now free from the tangle of blankets, felt pulled back into a new, more comfortable position. She unfolded her legs from beneath her; the mask seemed to make things easier, she felt lifted despite its weight.

Finally, she stood up in the trailer. She looked out of the eyeholes in the mask. There was no longer a joint between where the mask ended and her skin began. The sockets in the mask were her eye sockets, and her black-rimmed eyelids blinked, covering for a second the shiny black beads that were her eyes. People in the crowd turned to see her. Then the screaming began, first with her mother. The small crowd surged against itself. No one knew what to do, where to look. Some fell, some bowed down. Some burned.

The fire reflected gold in the sheen of her feathers as Matilda flapped her wings and soared.

3

--·--

FEATHERS

I n those days it was hot. Each summer hotter, wetter. I
was at school, aged nine. Deep and loyal friendships yet
to be discovered; still wanting to play games. My innocence
fully fledged.

At lunchtimes we played hopscotch. The faces at my side
now faded, their wide mouths less so.

Trees on the land nearby hummed with noise. White
blossoms amongst their branches rolled without a breeze;
Little Corellas.

They'd moved in a week or two before, thriving and
tearing at the bark with their long pointed beaks. I
remember the teacher telling us to stay away from them,
that they were dangerous vermin. They seemed harmless to
me.

The school bell rang, the birds were startled. A cloud of
white leapt from the trees towards us. Everything stopped

in the playground, we all looked up. Something was wrong, their noises different that afternoon, like little screams.

Thudding onto the ground beside me, on hopscotch number six, one of the flock. Blood streamed from its eyes and beak.

Then another on number one, its wings twisted beside its soft body at unnatural angles. Again, the red on the white, a vivid message.

There were shouts from the staff, telling us to go inside, to take cover. The corellas were dive-bombing us, reluctant kamikazes falling from the sky. They were everywhere on the ground. We stumbled over them back towards the school doors. Blood and feathers smeared across gingham uniforms. Tearful, once virtuous faces now beyond known experience.

The emergency services came, the birds were swept up and taken away to be burned.

For months after, guilt walked at my side and white feathers filled my nights.

4

— · —

EXUVIA

Reaching for the wardrobe door, my hand looks slick in the morning light. It delves inside as if not connected to me, going where the suits hang ready. Today is homeschool again. I peel my sleeping suit from my limbs and hang it on the padded satin hanger; that one is all about comfort. Then I shimmy the teacher suit from the wooden hook on the back of the door. This suit was comfortable back in my twenties but now it is tired, torn in parts, and a little too tight around my middle. Still, I must wear it for my two children at home today. I pull it around me and it clings. There is even a grasping, compressing sensation around my hands. It will cut my circulation off if I keep it on for too long.

My eyes are drawn to the suit hanging at the back of the rail and my heart flutters. It feels out of reach, like another life. I've not worn it in so long. Pulling the other suits forward a little along the rail, I take it out and hold it up. It

is soft and plump, and curves in places where I don't. It feels
new compared to the teacher one I have just put on.

I had just become accustomed to wearing this newer,
more curvaceous suit, on weekends away from my family,
then all this happened, the stuff outside. So I had to stop. I
slide the suit back in its place, it doesn't do me any good to
ponder on the past. Especially when I can't see a future
where I'm able to wear it again.

I get them up and make myself a coffee, pouring it down
my gullet; it scorches my oesophagus.

Later, I escape from being downstairs, seeking a moment
to myself and refusing to sit on the toilet again to get it. I
come back to my bedroom. The top drawer of my dresser is
slightly open as if to tempt me. I glance inside as I go to
push it closed, but it's too late. The sparkle of the trinkets
inside is a siren song. Don't save us for best, they whisper in
chorus. I slam it shut to keep them quiet, it works, or at least
I can't hear them anymore. When will I ever wear them
again?

The world beyond our front door is full of bodies, but
not like before. Insidious ideas that have been hidden for
generations have come back out, been pulled from the loft
or the basement, or the secret cabinet hidden in a wall, like a
fashion that repeats through time. You'd think these ideas
had gone away, these battles surely have been fought time
and time again. But identities get hidden away, just like my
favourite, waiting until there are enough with the same
feelings to become the zeitgeist. This moment is not for me.

Many are thriving on power trips. A part-time pharmacy assistant suddenly asked to work the front door, like a bouncer at a club. She has found her calling; a military career she never thought herself capable of. She can't wait to begin work each day. I don't go there anymore.

In this time anonymity is a thrilling tool. Bodies are saying and doing things they wouldn't have dared to vocalise or perform before. Now they are getting away with it. The polarity is palpable.

It's not safe, especially for someone like me, on the fringes and not easily put in a box. I never felt safe but now it is worse. But despite all this I need to be free, despite all this, I need to wear my favourite suit. To take the risks, because if I don't, I don't know what I'll do stuck in here with my family.

I make a pact with myself.

We finish early and I peel off the old suit and hang it back up. My flesh blooms where I've been compressed. I can breathe again, no longer vac-packed like a frozen salmon fillet. I reach for my favourite skin and slip it on. It's like an embrace from an old lover, home. My posture instantly changes, there's even a smile creeping onto my face. I pull the skin up tighter over my cheekbones to make my smile bigger. Then open the drawer and pull out some of the adornments that winked at me earlier. The rhinestone and feather headdress is the last to go on. It sits on my unbrushed, one-day-past-wash-day hair.

As I leave, I call out behind me. I don't know if they hear, but I shut the door anyway and begin my passage through the streets. My newly smooth and curvaceous thighs jiggle as I strut. I am becoming again.

It's not long before the first one arrives, grasping at me, hooking into my layers, their voice muffled behind their mask. Then another and another. I can feel the suit of skin I'm wearing loosen at my shoulders. I keep walking. Suddenly there is a freeing sensation, the grabbing is diminished and the cool air bites my exposed muscles and tendons. More alive than before, I look down and they have torn the skin from me. Only ribbons of it are left. Strips hang off my shoulders, swinging in the breeze between rhinestones. There's no blood, but I shine a deep shade of pink. This freedom takes my breath away.

5

QUEEN OF THE UNDERWORLD

Like a well-read book, I fall open on his favourite page. Words tumble from our mouths.

Lips electric. Eyes wide; They are cavern holes, luring, consuming every part of me, taking enough time. We merge our stories. His breath deep and steady, my heart like a starling in my chest. We peel back versions of each other to get to the inner truth. Like remembered rituals in a foreign language.

Our rivers intertwine as he leans over and buries his head into my neck. I'm lost to the mortal world, as he sinks deeper into the roots of me. Power warms within and without. I let him think he's reached my centre.

Crowned, now and always as Queen of the Underworld. My hands search for his head jigsaw clicked with my body, I pull and release it from my jugular. He has served his purpose.

I have an aversion to stasis. I am nauseous at small talk. I brood, then erupt. Reforming for the better. I am breezy about being underestimated, made out to be smaller, assumed to take up less space. I will show them soon enough.

Looking out onto the coast, the wind carries the cries from the stone slabs at the top of the hill. Here, a silky tail curls around him, a leathery paw pokes from beneath as he sleeps, curled in a ball. I nurture the seed. We are back from hell and we have changed. People pass and we are unseen. I do the inner work, becoming ready behind the invisible windows.

6

– · –

THE TREATMENT

In the round of the arena, black pumps settled on a
dusty floor and a face turned toward a canvas sky. He
was on the front row in his usual spot and in his usual state;
transfixed by the trapeze rehearsals. Despite his constant
gaze upwards, neck strain was never a problem for Pierrot.
Sometimes he brought a sketchbook and graphite. Clothed
in his loose costume, it was the only way his fellow
performers recognised him, the Clown. The white makeup
given a rest when not on duty.

"Have you nothing better to do, Pierrot?" Artem asked
him from above. Pierrot ignored the man, giving no sign he
had even heard the question.

This was the only thing for him to do. There was
nothing else. Other than being clean. Bathing was Pierrot's
first love. It had been too long since the last time. The folds
in his flesh were littered with a rash. Dusting powder no
longer enough to stave away the damp, or the smell. He'd

begged the boss to organise something for him at the next town. The next town was this one. He should go and check again. After the rehearsal that is exactly what he would do.

Below the trapezes, stagehands began setting up the spinning ring. The ring was a huge draw for the attendees of the circus. One of a kind; a metal frame that spun on the ellipse and was mounted on a support frame at either end. Tracks on the frame enabled the chair performers, whilst plenty of bars and joints supported the aerial silk team. A feat of mechanical engineering.

Pierrot sighed as the trapeze practice came to an end. Boris and Artem leapt down, they always made it look so easy. He watched them. Another heated debate. These were happening increasingly often. Artem wandered off but Boris came toward the clown. Pierrot sat up a little straighter and placed a smile on his face.

Don't come too close, my sweet. I don't want you to catch a whiff of the aroma I carry around.

Boris stopped as if he'd heard Pierrot's thoughts.

"Are you okay? You look a little strained today, is something bothering you?"

"I'm alright. Thank you for asking though."

Boris nodded in acknowledgement and continued past him and outside.

Right then, nothing left but to remind the boss about his dire need. He rose slowly from the seat, the faster he moved the more smell he'd give off. Even his gowns had started to yellow, especially around the crotch and armpit areas. He was alternating three of the costumes but they all needed a deep clean. Some of the knees and elbows were grubby and he didn't know what else to do.

His place in the hierarchy of the circus was low. Very low. He needed permission for everything. Onward to the boss's office. To Pierrot's surprise, the boss was expecting him.

Gemini Bathhouse; someone would be waiting for him there. He was to bring all his clothes for laundering. Everything. Excitement filled Pierrot's bones as he packed his costumes into a bag. The boss said there were steam rooms, an exfoliating treatment, and a massage he could look forward to. Pierrot became aroused thinking about the touch he longed for. The pressure of palms on his body. He was overdue for this treatment and the boss knew it. That would explain why it seemed so indulgent this time.

Pierrot left his caravan, making sure he had the map within one of his pockets. This time the circus was set up on a wasteland outside a greying town. He wore his only set of civilian clothing. The boss didn't like townies making connections to the performers, Pierrot hated these clothes.

"Going somewhere nice, P?" Artem shouted from the backstage area that grew outside at every town. The performers' caravans formed layers of concentric circles around a bonfire. Most would bring out camping tables and chairs to sit and chat between performances. Pierrot never joined them.

"I'm off on an errand," he shouted back to nosy Artem.

Pierrot quickened his pace and found himself within the grey town sooner than he'd expected. He looked down at

the map his boss had given him. He was close, the
bathhouse was on this side of town.

Today is my day, everything is going my way.

He had five hours before the performance later that
night. Plenty of time to get himself back up to scratch. He
was going to enjoy himself. As if on cue, it was there again:
the excitement clutching at him, and that feeling deep
inside his pelvis.

The place was two streets away. The town was quiet,
only labourers milled about getting food from street
vendors. The shops and restaurants must be on the opposite
side of town, he thought. The land is always cheaper to rent
on the rougher edges, it was the same everywhere.

He arrived. Hardly able to contain himself he reached to
ring the bell, but a voice stopped him.

"Pierrot, wait. You don't have to do this."

He turned to see Boris a few steps behind.

"What? Why? You followed...?" Pierrot felt confused but
flattered. What was Boris doing?

"You don't have to do this. I'm sorry for following you,
but I can't stand back and watch this again."

*So that's what the arguments were about with Artem.
He's losing it, not cut out for a life on the road.*

The civilian clothes enhanced the acrobat's beauty rather
than diminished it; Boris couldn't even pretend to be
normal.

"Boris, I'm overdue some TLC that's all this is. Nothing
else." He congratulated himself for not stumbling over his
words. A truck trundled down the grey street, its inhabitant

leaning out to get a better view of Boris. Pierrot wasn't like other men, not like that anyway.

"Do you think I followed you here to stop you from having a wash? Don't you see, Pierrot, it's more than that, what they do here... in these places..."

"I've never been to this town before, I'm pretty sure you haven't either..."

"It's a set-up, I know the boss's scams. How long have you been in this circus?"

Pierrot paused, his finger still above the doorbell, "Longer than you," he pushed down. The bell reverberated into the walls beyond. The siren call of the bathhouse overwhelmed him. The thought of a clean body, face, feet, costume all too delectable. A buzzer sounded and Pierrot pushed the door open. He looked over his shoulder at Boris. "I'll be fine, see you tonight. I'll be looking up for you."

"I'm sorry. I should've told you sooner, I wanted to—"

The pleading faded as Pierrot made his way into the building. He followed the signs pointing downstairs. The humid air hit him along the staircase. The smell of tea tree, lavender, then camphor filled his nostrils. He began to perspire, the itch, the folds of his skin covered with sores, screamed at him. He hoped the staff here could help. He hoped he wouldn't disgust them.

"How are you doing today?" A man dressed in blue cotton at a desk at the bottom of the stairs asked Pierrot.

"I'm okay, excited to be here," the clown replied. "My boss arranged for me to attend today, I am Pierrot."

"Yes, we have you here on the schedule. Welcome!"

The corners of Pierrot's mouth turned upward as his shoulders relaxed. He left his laundry at the desk and followed the man to the changing area.

"Someone will come and collect you shortly. Put one of these on." The man pulled a white waffle cotton robe from a shelf where they were folded on top of one another. Pierrot wanted to touch them. They were so white, so perfect; so clean. The man left Pierrot alone, leaving behind a fresh, grassy aroma. The clown made a mental note to ask for its name on the way out, he'd love to smell like that every day. If it were sold somewhere nearby he could go home via the perfumery.

The changing room was all terrazzo. Four cubicles on one side and a long row of benches opposite with mirrors above. He didn't bother with a cubicle, being here alone, there was no point. He tugged at his civilian clothes and shoes and placed them on the bench.

Standing straight, he examined himself in the mirror; his beastly skin marbled with the pinky-red rash. A wave of worry washed over him; what if the treatments here stung, what if they made his skin worse? He couldn't bear the reflection any longer and grabbed the robe. As he put it on he realised it was far too small for him. He went back to the shelf near the door to try and find one in a bigger size. He felt sick. This should be an enjoyable experience. There was a knock at the door.

"I'm not quite ready yet," Pierrot said as he rifled through the robes. He took one that seemed bigger and put it on. It was still on the small side, but at least this overlapped and covered him up. Opening the door, he found the therapist waiting for him.

"Sorry about that, I had some issues with the robe."

"No problem, you aren't wearing it for long so there are no problems." The therapist had an accent he didn't recognise. They walked down the corridor and then directed Pierrot into a shadowy, small room.

"We start with massage." The therapist explained. "You strip, lie face down on the treatment table. Put your face through this hole. This towel is for your modesty but I'll be moving it around as I work on your body."

"Thank you," was all Pierrot managed to say. The therapist left the room. Pierrot trembled as he hung the robe up and climbed onto the table, following the instructions exactly. He lay there grateful for being on his front, the anticipation was almost too much to bear.

The warm room made him sweat, the itchy crevices of his skin pleading for attention. He gazed at the floor below the table, his features squashed into the face cradle. A knock at the door and the therapist reentered.

"You are here to relax, I will help you."

"Thank you." Saliva dropped out of his mouth onto the tiles below as he tried to speak.

"You don't need to talk."

He felt a pair of hot, damp towels on his neck. They pushed along his spine and down to his buttocks. It gave him goosebumps, his skin felt alive where they'd passed over. Then again, this time from the tops of his shoulders down his torso, over his ribcage and to his waist.

He flinched. "Sorry, I'm a little ticklish there."

"No worries. We need to loosen you up." The therapist ran the towels over him more delicately this time. Then collected fresh ones for cleaning his arms and legs.

"Now we start the massage. We fix this rash for you."

The kneading began. Around his neck at first, then across his shoulders. There were lots of knots, lots of clicking. The borders between pain and pleasure blurred. He felt the therapist's elbow under his shoulder blades loosening things up.

The therapist brushed down his arms and legs with a steaming body brush. He couldn't tell if his skin was stinging anymore, everything felt on fire.

"Now we do your facial. Roll over, please."

Pierrot did as instructed. He covered his enlarged groin with the towel and closed his eyes, waiting for the more precise work on his face. It was then he felt a needle in his neck, his eyes sprang open and he tried to get up.

"Don't worry, this is normal. You'll be fine in a moment. You won't feel a thing."

The therapist held him down, he was losing any power he'd had. He couldn't feel his hands, nor could he tell if he was even breathing. The numbness travelled quickly through his body. He tried wiggling his toes and then he was out.

A second therapist came in dressed in similar clinical scrubs. They wheeled in a tray of surgical tools and a large bin.

"Is he slackened?" They prodded Pierrot's abdomen.

"Yes, very loose now. It shouldn't be a problem removing this one."

"Good work, this a hide replacement only, they want him to keep everything else."

"We still remove some memories though, right?"

"Yes, yes of course. Let's begin." They worked with a skill that came from repetition. The therapists sliced into Pierrot and removed his skin. Every part of his epidermis was peeled away, revealing a milky, near-transparent flesh. Underneath was a steely mechanical structure: Pierrot's skeleton.

"The silicone is starting to rupture."

"That explains the rash, we should seal that. We'll have to add it to the bill." They set about their work, Pierrot's old skin was thrown in the bin and its replacement wheeled in.

Later, Pierrot woke up on a lounger. The robe around him, fitted him like it had been made to measure. He must have dozed off. He felt groggy, but oh so clean. The therapist came in, smiling this time.

"I was about to come and wake you. It's time you were getting back to the circus, there's sure to be a queue forming."

"Thanks. Yes, I was wondering what time it was."

"Your things have are all laundered and are waiting for you in the changing rooms. We cleaned everything you brought with you."

"Wonderful, thanks for everything."

"No problem."

At least he wouldn't smell anymore. He was ashamed for letting it get as bad as it had. He dressed in the clean, civilian clothing and packed away the costumes. He headed back to the circus site, consulting the map more than he'd care to admit.

Artem spotted him arriving back into the camp and came straight over.

"Have you seen Boris? He's not come back yet."

"Come back from where?" Pierrot said.

"Didn't he leave with you earlier?"

"No, I haven't seen him since this morning when you two were arguing."

"Yes, of course. You're feeling much better now? You look it."

"I am like a new man," Pierrot said as Artem turned away. "Are you worried about Boris? Does the boss know he's missing?"

"Yes, and no. I'd better go and tell him."

Pierrot got back to his caravan and put his bag on the table inside. He went to the mirror and pulled off the T-shirt. His skin was beautiful, so smooth, there was no sign of the rash, nor the odour from before. The bathhouse had performed a miracle. Something did smell though, the caravan needed a clean. He hung the costumes up and opened the windows wide. There was an hour before the performance time.

As dusk fell the music of the circus boomed through the speaker system for the waiting guests. Pierrot put on one of his laundered costumes. It no longer irritated his skin. The caravan was clean and his face painted back to its chalky Clown White. Everything felt right again. Sitting back down at his dressing table he started to attach the ruff around his neck and heard a tap at the door.

"It's open," he called out, as he fiddled with the fasteners. The small door to the caravan swung open and in stepped Boris.

"Good evening, Pierrot."

"They found you then?"

"I don't know what you mean. I've not been anywhere." He sat down and put his head in his hands.

"That's exactly what I said. Artem tried to tell me you'd come with me to the Baths." Pierrot finally fastened up the ruff at the back of his neck and looked up at Boris through the mirror. He looked beautiful; covered in gold sequins with scarlet feathers entwined in his black curls. Was he crying?

"I'm scared, Pierrot. My head feels strange, I thought you might have some painkillers here." He lifted his head off his hands and swooned, then his chin began to judder. He tried to speak but it was gibberish. Pierrot turned on his chair as Boris's nose began to bleed. His body slid off the small cushioned caravan settee and began convulsing. He banged his head on a cupboard on the way down to the floor, scraping the side of his face up to the ear.

Pierrot jumped off his chair and tried to lift him onto the seat again. The acrobat's head lolled around on his neck. Pierrot called out for help while Boris convulsed in his arms and the gold sequins flew everywhere, covering the inside of

the caravan. Then Pierrot saw the scrape had caused the ear
to be severed from Boris's head. He stopped convulsing.
Pierrot knew no one was coming. No one had heard him
over the loudspeakers. He placed Boris's body on the settee
and stood. Blood covered the front of his costume and the
sequins clung to the red like stars in a claret sky.

7

—·—

BACK FOR SECONDS

He goes out to the forest every day in summer, laying foundations. The most important bit, he says. He won't tell her exactly where it is in the forest, but she knows it must be beside the river. He will need water to mix the cement or whatever he's using for the base. It must also be close enough to the road for the delivery of materials.

She watches him wander down the path and into the layers of green beyond their chalet. Gone for the day, but only when the weather is fair. On rainy days, they get under each other's feet, argue and bicker. When he's gone, she feels like she can breathe. Yesterday she noticed she was singing. It took her a moment to realise what the sound was.

She sits out back when he's not there. She has something slow cooking on the stove for supper, but she likes it out back. The light is good for quilting, her eyes not being as good as they were. It can take a while to thread a needle indoors by candlelight. He's always refused to apply for electricity, he says joining the grid would mean their lives wouldn't be private anymore, reckons governments and such will be able to track them that way, see their movements somehow. She sits there and works; the birds are almost tame, swishing and swashing in the nearby birdbath. It takes about two weeks to make a quilt, or it used to. Lately, she has been slower. The fabric isn't coming through as fast as it once had. She's not moaning about it; her fingers don't work that quick anymore either. But he gets upset, the quilts bring in money. He takes them and sells them at the market.

The breeze brushes her white hair around her face, like a cloud. On it, the smell of something sweet, like a fairground; candy floss, coconut ice, sugar in every form. Those candy colours are always so attractive to children. Not the colours of the quilt she is working on. It is nasty. In colour and in smell. The fabric is old and worn, and the bloodstains are stubborn. It is all they could get lately, so she pushes through the wickedness. They need the money and there's always someone who will buy.

The sun chair creaks as she leans back, scrunching up her eyes at the sky and the tree line. It's in these moments, near the end of one quilt and the hopeful start of another, she questions her happiness. She knows too well that if she were truly happy, these thoughts wouldn't even come up. But she's always been the analytical sort. That was her old job, before she met him. She was smitten back then. Sometimes still so, like when he brings something special for supper along with some colourful, fresh-smelling fabrics.

He was so vulnerable back then, a widower grieving for a wife she only knows as G. They'd been childhood sweethearts, he'd told her. Growing up together, taking this place over together from the one who lived here before. When she'd died, he'd come to town, looking for a new wife, she now realised. But he'd enchanted her with promises of escaping the rat race. She'd insisted on a rebuild, to put their own mark on a place. That's what he had been working on, continuing the self-sustainability he was so proud of. But the fact he's not letting her see? She toys with the idea it might be him trying to be romantic, but that, too, is rare these days.

She has considered following him one morning, but her mobility isn't great. He would hear and they'd argue again, which she hates. Either that or she'd fall. They are so remote no one would find her until it's too late, and she'd be eaten by the night animals. He says he's doing it for her and he will take her to see it once it's finished. She has lost track of how long it's been. She loses track of lots of things. Her brain must be shrinking in on itself. The quilts are the only thing that keeps her going. She drifts into a sleep where she can walk around the world.

Hours later, she wakes with the cold setting in her bones. The birds have gone quiet, and it's growing dark. He'll be back soon, and he'll tell her off again for falling asleep outside. Shivering, she heaves herself and the quilt from the chair and clings to the wall as she hobbles in through the back door. The food smells ready. She pulls on her housecoat, another quilted creation, from back when there was an excess of fabric. It is soft and comforting. She lays the table, sure that there are only minutes to spare. Candles are lit and the back door is locked. It feels later than usual. And then he's there, all bluster and dust through the door.

"Smells good!"

"Are you later tonight?" She puts out the bowls on the worktop and lifts the lid of the pan with a quilted oven mitt.

"Aye, a little. I was waiting on a delivery." He pulls his knapsack from the floor where he'd dropped it and loosens the drawstring opening, fishing around with his big hands inside the canvas. "Here." A pile of patterned cotton fabric emerges. He puts them on the table.

"Oh, Hansel. I was only thinking I needed some new pieces earlier. Thank you." She brings over the bowls of stew and they eat, her eyes straying to the pile of fabric throughout the meal. Finally, pushing the bowl to one side, she lifts them up to her nose, inhaling the fabric.

"I could smell this on the air today," she says. "This sweetness. You aren't far from here, are you."

It isn't a question, and yet she waits for a response.

"Not far."

She stands, and her chair topples over behind her. He sighs and reaches down, lifting it back into place.

"I'll show you soon. Promise."

"When is soon?" She fumbles through her sewing kit on a shelf by the back door. She wants to give the impression she is casually asking, but they both know she is not. "Ah-

ha! Here they are." She lifts the pinking shears up in the air
like a trophy and returns to sit at the table.

Hansel slurps at his spoon, keeping his eyes focused on a
knot in the wood of the tabletop. The candles flicker as she
goes through the pile of fabric, bringing it all to her lap and
lifting each one piece by piece. She snips off the collars and
the sleeves, the waistbands and the cuffs, deconstructing
each item until a new pile appears of sheared flattened
fabric, ready for quilting.

8

THE CARER

Filling the pan halfway with milk, then three handfuls of oats, maybe more. I never measure out the ingredients, always doing it by eye.

You are standing there waiting for me; at the end of the aisle, the start of our new life.

The pan goes on the hob and I light the gas with a match. Our ignition is no longer sparking. Stirring gently, the circles become the rhythm of my breath.

I take the steps and I'm standing alongside you. Your eyes are cloudy and I didn't know then, but that was the start of it all.

The porridge begins to bubble. I stir faster ensuring none gets stuck to the bottom of the pan. A little splashes out and I tell myself to stay calm, to slow down.

Our first night as husband and wife you spilled over into me, convincing me we were happy.

Now your oats are smooth and creamy. I read recently, something linking them to increased libido; a claim I've yet to witness as fact. I get your favourite bowl, releasing your breakfast into it, then reach for the baby spoon, adding it to the tray. There's no golden syrup today, I've found a new sweetener; ethylene glycol. Sitting alongside you on the bed my heart races.

"Breakfast time," I say, stirring the mixture together. You open your eyes, opaque like the porridge. I load the spoon and steady myself.

9

THE HUM

The heat is suffocating. I throw off my side of the duvet and the chilly air hits the dampness of the t-shirt I sleep in. It's like I'm glued to the bed with my own sweat. It's an effort to roll onto my side and I fight the temptation to grab my phone to check the time. If I keep my eyes half-closed, I will drop off again after a trip to relieve my bladder and change my t-shirt. I don't want to get stuck within the rectangular glow again, so I peel myself up, skin like wet paper.

My partner, Stanley, is oblivious to my turmoil as I cling to the wall then the banister. We moved here a few weeks ago and I'm not yet accustomed to the shape of it in the dark. There are a couple of steps down to the bathroom. I feel for them with my feet, looking for the light from outside. I make it and close the door behind me as quietly as I can, shivering in the sweat-soaked t-shirt. It was only

minutes ago I was certain you'd be able to fry an egg on my
chest.

The house backs onto a train line. The floodlights glow
all night, accompanying any moon that is out. The toilet
seat is cold. I forget about keeping my eyes half-closed and
my brain half asleep. Instead, I open the blinds a little more
and gaze up at the platform, higher than the roof of our
terrace house. I had worried about train crashes before we'd
finally agreed to buy this one. What if a train came off the
rails, sliding off the embankment and crashing into the
house? We wouldn't stand a chance if it was one of those
cargo trains which race through the station at high speeds.
The house, and us in it, would all be crushed.

The platform itself is long, so long there is never anyone
this far down. If there was, they'd have a perfect view of me
sitting on the toilet. The embankment turns into our back
garden and between our garden and the track grow saplings
and ferns. There are trees that have come down in the wind
here too, layered with leaves and time. The local cats fight,
hunt, and spy on one another in this undergrowth.

The bathroom door juts open and in strolls our cat, Poe.
He loves to watch: the little weirdo. There's a movement
outside, along with the wail of another catfight. Poe hears it
and I lift the blinds up fully for us both to get a closer look.
He jumps onto the windowsill and we look out together,
searching the pockets of light and the blurred edges of the
garden we've only just begun to know. I can't see anything,
but Poe fixes on something out there. It must be his arch-
nemesis from two doors down, his back arches and I go to

close the blind, sleep and a dry t-shirt suddenly calling me. He hisses and brings a paw up to the window and I wonder whether it's his own reflection he's getting mad about.

"Come on, stop messing."

A low hum emits from his body and I pull the blind down. Then he launches himself out of the bathroom and thunders down the stairs like a mad thing. I wash my hands and head back to bed, groping around in the dark. I find the t-shirt Stanley had on during the day and swap my wet one for his dry. In bed I lie there annoyed at Poe as I experiment with how dark the room is with my eyes open compared to when my eyes are closed; there's not much difference. The humming grows louder and I grope around the duvet to feel for the cat. He must have followed me in here. But there are only handfuls of cotton, my other half's hip, and no Poe.

I'm wide awake, so just one look, to see what time it is. Then I'll know how long I've got left to sleep and if it's even worth it. I reach over to my bedside and feel for the slender device. Discovering the cool edges, I lift it and turn it to face me. 3:11. The glow shines in my palm as if shooting a laser into the back of my skull.

The hum is still there, but I can't tell if it's definitively here with me. It's probably not even in the house. More likely to be coming from outside, probably something to do with the trains. I try to ignore it and have a quick look at a property listings site for anything new. Scrolling houses I can't afford always seems to help me drift off to sleep.

The next day, Stanley is up and out early for a run, I feel him kiss me on the head and whisper a promise of coffee on his return. But the hum is still there and I can't get back to sleep. Bleary-eyed and barefooted in my dressing gown, I let Poe out whilst I have breakfast and I notice the hum disappears. I switch on the radio and the hum is back, now coming out of the speaker. The DJ talks over the top.

"Last night, there were reports of a strange noise. What you can hear right now is a recording of it from one of our listeners. NASA has released a statement saying it could be interstellar gas, vibrating within the earth's atmosphere. Some are saying it's aliens. What do you think? Did you hear it? Call us now, we can get you live on air."

The insipid jingle follows, and I think about calling into the show. What would Stanley say? I should ask him first. Cereal crunches as I shovel it into my mouth and I hear Poe scratching at the door. The chair scrapes the wooden floor as I slide it back and stand to let the contrary creature back in. As I open the door, he darts past my legs and yowls, a sound I've never heard him make. Then I see, on the stone slabs of the yard from where Poe has just returned. Stanley lies there, collapsed in the backyard after his run. He is facing away from me. I move to step out of the narrow patio doors but I'm stopped in my tracks by the hum. Louder than before, coming from the radio, from Poe, from Stanley's body. I retreat and stumble backwards, the table stopping me from falling down. There's something wet on the floor, between my toes, my brain assumes it's cat sick and I must call an ambulance. Call someone. The hum is hurting my ears like it is burrowing into my brain.

I turn back, look for my phone on the table beside my bowl. But Poe is there, larger than before with a strange look in his eye and his mouth slightly ajar. He's sat in something wet, and his coat is gleaming with slime. I grab my phone and turn to go out into the yard. I step into the wetness again, then I'm slammed down onto the floor. My head hits the table edge this time and my phone clatters as it splinters. Woozy. I must get away from this noise. It feels like there's a slicked rope holding my ankles. I try and lift my head to see what it is. Something heavy and wet slides over me and into the house. Is it Stanley? I am numb. All I can hear is my cat purring.

10

—— ◇ ——

TUBULAR

I nside a heart, something grows. This heart is small.
Much smaller than yours. This heart is within a jack
jumper ant queen and she is oblivious to the change.
Instinct is all she knows. Her nest is in the sandy soil at the
base of a tree so old, it has split in half. No one knows it is
still growing.

The zoo has been built around this ancient tree. Its roots
are too deep and far-reaching to consider removing. An easy
home for the jack jumpers, far away enough from the
barriers and the rest of the zoo to prevent harm, but close
enough for study. Their sting venom is precious, individual
to each ant like each has its own version of the recipe.

The season is hot and dry, like most summers now. Inside
the nest, beneath the tree, the queen is overheating. The
thing growing in her heart wants to get out. Her red and
black segmented body strains. The impotent wings on her

back vibrate and her long mandibles rub against each other like a cook sharpening knives.

Poised. Waiting.

A shadow passes over the top of the nest. She sends soldiers out to defend her. They leap and soar, happy to be given freedom from their tasks. While they are away she devours the eggs in the cosmos-like colony and grows bigger. An ant's heart isn't like a human's. It is more like a vein, a tubular thing which, in this case, has a parasite hitching a lift, craving space and a life of its own. The thing inside is the last of its kind and was put inside the queen by a messenger from the other worlds when she was larvae.

She squeezes her heavy body through the chambers of the nest to the surface. Seeing her soldiers covering a felled beast, she is compelled to lie down on a rock, the heat is unforgiving. Beneath her exoskeleton tiny explosions occur, the thing inside feeds on the eggs the queen has consumed. A hairline fracture appears on the abdomen of the queen's body. Her head tips back, mandibles slicing the air. Another crack, this time larger, and the queen stops moving. There is a hatching from her carcass. A long wet creature slips from the space it has forced open. It unfolds itself; twice the size of the queen it was housed in. It needs liquid, it has its own eggs to lay.

A flurry of blue lands on the rock beside the queen, it cocks its head and looks at the little worm-like thing, then lifts it from the rock with its beak. It takes flight again over the zoo and visitors stand and point as it lands in the children's play area.

11

Night Revelations

There were no fences around the runway back then. Just trees and bush enough to put folk off wandering. People feared the roaring noise from the aeroplanes, tending to stay away. But not the younger population, they felt differently. It was a badge of honour if you went there and could prove it. Only the rich kids had the Polaroid cameras, though, so already they were well ahead of us, a different starting line.

On the night in question, I'd been working at a local pub. Flirting with the punters increased my tip jar. It helped that some of them wanted to bed me, even the married ones. I always brushed it off, just part of their fantasy and part of my job. My performance for their night out. I seemed naïve, but I saw them as harmless.

My friends were at the pub that night. I'd pretend to get them both drunk by giving them extra shots in their drinks, another barmaid perk. It wasn't long before one group of lads cottoned on that Gill and Alice were my mates, and started chatting them up. It was weird to watch them all as an outsider. The group of lads were older than us, but some we recognised from school. A familiar face here and there. "My brother was in your year," stuff like that. There was a lot of banter. I wished I hadn't been working, but I was the glue attaching these two factors together. It felt powerful.

Alice came over for more drinks. She asked if I had a preference over which one she copped off with. It was nice to be asked; she didn't normally. I said I didn't care, leaving fate to sort it out. In reality, of course, I wanted the tall, quiet one if the opportunity presented itself. She didn't need to know that. It would be a test for him too if she wanted him and he rebuffed her. That would make him more attractive, someone with the ability to say no to Alice.

When I rang the bell for last orders, I caught Alice's eye. She was over at the other end of the bar, near the pot wash and the steam from the machine floated up and across her. It gave her a look of a pagan deity at some kind of ritual. She just needed a flower crown. Her eyes pleaded. Her mouth shaped words. I knew what she meant. We'd been invited to go somewhere after the pub shut, somewhere with the lads. I'd had plenty of these offers during my months of working there, but never one where my friend had been the messenger. I'd stayed for the occasional lock-in, but it was never much fun playing catch up with some punters, even if they were all buying my drinks. Adrenaline fizzed in my chest as I stood there, my hand still on the bell cord. I bought some time, shrugging my shoulders. Alice rolled her eyes and waved her empty glass at me.

"I've saved the lanky one for you," she told me as I sorted out their order.

"Shut up." I blushed and decided to go with them. It had been a while since my last conquest.

The pub had a bowling green that backed onto some farmland, which then turned into a golf course, then the scrub and trees around the runway. As the crow flies, the end of the runway was around three miles away. They were all waiting for me outside in the car park. It was early September, and the nights were still warm and long. I was driving, and it turned out the tall, quiet lad was too, so the group split between our two cars and I said I'd trail him. It was quickly apparent where we were going. There were two lads in my car in the back with Alice. Gill was in the front with me.

"Have you been before?" they asked me.

"To the end of the runway? Yes."

"When did you go?" Alice said from behind me, drunk. "I think she's pulling your legs, lads."

I caught her eye in the rear-view mirror and glared.

"I'd like to pull yours," the one who sat next to her said as he started kissing her neck.

The drive was along the edges of the golf course, overhung with trees marking the boundary, and the lanes were narrow. It was more direct to walk, as I had done in the past, but never this late. I could see that the lad I liked, let's call him Tom, was as careful a driver as I was. I held back

from his car in case an animal jumped into the road and he
needed to brake.

Gill had put the car radio on and was singing along to
Teenage Dirtbag. She was pretty good. I followed the car in
front as it bore left and down a tiny track. Perfect, I'd be the
first to reverse out later. A part of me wished I'd gone home.
I was still in my work uniform and practical, unattractive
shoes. After parking, I flipped open a compact from my
handbag, pressed some powder into the shine on my
forehead, wiped the flakes of mascara off my cheeks and
reapplied some lipstick.

"You look f-iii-ne!" Gill sang to me. Alice was snogging
her guy in the back seat by then. Gill got out and the other
lad, sat behind her, did too. They walked to the car in front
whose inhabitants were all piling out into the night, plastic
bags clinking with bottles. My tummy rumbled.

"I'll leave you to it, Alice," I said. She let him kiss her
neck again and as I climbed out, she held two thumbs up
behind his head, through the already steamy window. I
chuckled; he had no idea what he was in for.

Underfoot was soft but not muddy as I joined the others.
There were five blokes from which Gill had her pick. She
knew by then I wanted Tom. He had beautiful eyes. One
lad rushed past me, with something in his hand. I turned as
a flash of light came from him. He held a Polaroid camera
aimed toward the back seat of my car. I wondered if he'd
just get the light reflecting off the window or what he
wanted, a picture of Alice. She was always discreet, there
was no need to worry. The camera whirred as it ejected the

square of paper. He put the picture in his pocket without even looking at it.

"They develop better in the warmth," he said as he rejoined us.

We walked through the undergrowth; the glow of the runway lighting was enough to see where we were going. The ground was cold, but we sat close enough to the end of the runway to see each other's faces and still be sheltered by the woodland on the other side. It was empty, as it was on my previous visits. A couple of wine bottles and a lonely boot lay bleakly at the treeline. Two of the lads rolled joints. I felt awkward in that stupid skirt I had to wear for work. Tom brought me over a bottle of beer, told me it was low alcohol and us drivers should stick together. I agreed and pretended to sip at the beer. Opposite me, Gill stood and played the five blokes off against each other, getting them to do challenges to prove their worthiness, her being the prize.

"I wish we could light a fire," one lad said.

"You know we can't, might cause problems with the aircraft," I replied.

"You said you'd been here before?" he said.

"Yeah?" Tom asked, turning to face me. "There's me thinking we were corrupting you…" He leaned in, closer to me. I could see his irises. The sharp, icy blue contrasted with the pinkness of the blood vessels in the whites of his eyes. His cheeks flushed as I let my gaze linger a little too long to be comfortable. I smiled, softening my intensity.

"A lady never tells," I said.

"So there are stories, then?" He was hooked. It was disappointingly easy, as usual. But by then I'd committed, and I still wanted to bide my time. There was no need to rush. I looked over at Gill. She had a joint in her hand and was blowing her inhaled smoke into one of the lads' faces. He was loving it, breathing it in, his eyes shut as if in submission. Gill and I locked eyes over the smoke, and in that exchange, we knew our next steps.

"We are going to play a game, Tom. Do you want to join us, or are you being looked after?" Gill handed me the joint.

"I'm alright, ta. Watch yourself with those drunken monkeys."

"I can handle myself." She spun around, turning her back to us. The five lads were like puppies waiting to be played with. "Let's play hide and seek. I'll count, you lot hide. When I find you, you will get a prize, but don't make it too easy or it's no fun."

They all scampered off into the undergrowth. She stood tall, backlit by the floodlights of the runway, her face in shadow. She counted loudly. I turned towards Tom. He stared at Gill, exposing his clean-shaven neck. The bit where a man's scalp turns to neck and ear. The veins lay there, thick, young, unfettered.

"You don't want one of Gill's prizes then?" I said.

"You aren't what I expected. Anyway, I've got the best prize, right here." He turned and looked me straight in the eye again. I did my best bashful giggle and batted my eyelashes. He took the joint from me, took a drag, then let it rest on top of a bottle.

"I really want to kiss you," he said.

"Well, get over here then." I retorted. He laughed, then we kissed. It was nice as kisses go. I remember reaching up to his head with my hands and running my fingers through his baby-soft hair. I could hear Gill still counting. I let him kiss my neck and waited for her to reach fifty.

"Coming, ready or not!" she shouted. I moved Tom's head with my hands so his eyes were in prime position. I let the instincts of my kind takeover; my body knew what to do. The venom was hot in my jawbone. I moved back from him, created some distance, unbuttoning, inviting him to see more of me. Made it so he couldn't take his beautiful eyes away. A smile spread across his face as he reached out. My timing was flawless. I cocked my head back, opened my mouth, and released the venom laced liquid-silk; it looked like silly string flying through the air. It began to set and congeal immediately on reaching Tom's face, sealing his mouth and nose. His looked even more delicious than before.

Gill grinned at me and disappeared into the trees. The 23:50 flight from Paris went over, and made everything vibrate; hiding the screams.

12

MILK

Our milkman drops the milk off between our garage and the parked car, hidden from view of the street. Threatened milk. The milk is safe there until I come to fetch it in before breakfast.

One morning the snow arrives and I go in my wellies, out to the white universe. The area where I'm collecting the milk is, in part, sheltered from the snow by the front of the car. This morning there are tracks on the drive; going in the same direction I am, toward the milk. The tracks are slight, non-human, non-cat, even smaller.

The snow crunches underfoot, making me noisier than I'd like, but I still see it. Something with fur. White fur supping at the milk. My milk. It is oblivious, in ecstasy and doesn't notice me despite my size and clumsiness. Then the spell breaks, it sees me as I lean in for a closer look. It is like a monkey but that's impossible. Its fur is the same shade of white as the milk and the snow. As I look it dissolves into a trillion pieces and merges with the milk. It pours itself into the full-fat bottle it drank from. It becomes milk. The foil cap sits on the snow by the side of my car, the only real evidence our milk has been tampered with. The creature is gone.

I bend and lift both bottles, bringing them inside. Careful not to spill. My kids already have the cereal out in their bowls. Eyes and mouths ready. I put their milk on the table and walk to the fridge, to get my own, oat milk because I'm allergic to the other. By the time I turn back they both have poured out their full-fat white fur onto their cereal and I don't say anything. The snow encroaches on the house.

13

—·—

DARK IS THE WATER

The rolling waves are gentle on my toes. Smooth grey
pebbles give my bare feet a massage I hadn't noticed
they needed. The horizon glows, the sun just saying its
goodbyes; the beach is empty, everyone inside because of
the curfew. The water reaches around the black cloth at my
ankles, no doubt leaving a salt mark there. I best go, I need
to move. Turning away from the water, it is a few steps to
the boots and socks I'd carefully placed a short distance
behind me, where the beach is more sandy, tucked in next
to a couple of rock pools. Leaning on the edge of one rock, I
dust off my feet before pulling on my socks. I must
continue my rounds. I cannot keep getting distracted by the
sunsets.

The sky is growing purple, almost navy. A slim reflection
of the moon shines in the rock pool at my side. I fasten my
boots and stand. Mind attempting to coax the body to
continue to carry on. I'm getting paid for checking people

are where they're supposed to be, not gazing at the ocean. A ripple snags at the corner of my eye. There's something in the rock pool, perhaps waiting for the tide to come back in. The moon's reflection wiggles at me again and I step closer, leaning in. The rock pool is long and narrow, around half a meter by perhaps two. Whatever it is, it's been waiting all day. I lean further, using an arm to brace myself against the rock. It is really dark now and I'm blocking the moon's reflection in the pool. The water looks black, like blood at night. I watch as my hand moves closer and before I know it, my fingers are breaking the surface of the black, flicking the liquid like a child might do to tease their parents.

Something attaches to my index finger with a tiny mouth, like a stapler. My finger throbs as I shake and flick to release the grip. It doesn't shift. I bash my finger against the rock and swear like a sailor. The thing won't budge. I can barely see what it is, but I grab it with my other hand and try to pull it off. It's wet, hard, and textured with tiny bristles like a cat's tongue. It doesn't move. I hold my hand against one of the lower rocks, then bring my foot up and crush it with my boot, like stepping on a snail in the rain.

I shake my throbbing, wounded hand hard, ridding myself of any detritus, then run up the beach awkwardly on the sand, toward the orange of the streetlights at the edge of the town. Standing under one of the amber lamps, I look at my hand. The black-red of blood is everywhere.

My finger, miraculously, is still intact, still all there, just bleeding. I call it in. Someone will come and collect me. I'll say it was a dog or something. They'll bandage me up and drop me at home.

The attendant at the medical centre knew I was lying about the dog. I think he liked me so said nothing. We just exchanged a look as he signed me off for a week. He attached a splint to my fingers and told me to keep it dry. The shard of shell or coral that he'd pulled from my finger it was given to me in an envelope like a prize, along with a tetanus booster and two stitches. My neighbour, Vera, from across the hall called round earlier with some soup. She's an old woman; lovely, but possibly senile. She said I looked different.

I keep looking in the mirror and there is something different about me, my reflection, but I can't place it. Maybe I've lost some weight. Maybe I've got an infection.

The pain wakes me. My finger still throbs and it feels like the swelling is increasing against the stitches, the splint and bandage. Perhaps I've just slept on it funny. My eyes are crusted with hardened sleep, which I try unsuccessfully to pick out of my eyelashes. I stagger to the bathroom as sunlight cuts through the gaps in my closed eyelids. I forgot to close the blind. Fumbling for a face cloth, I run it under the tap until it warms up and rub my eyes free. They feel swollen, like my finger. Puffy, and the fine skin filled with fluid, like an allergic reaction.

I pull on the plastic sandwich bag over the half of my hand covered by bindings and fasten it in place with an elastic band. Rest, that's all I need to do. Why do I find it so difficult?

The shower is just what the doctor ordered. I think of the medic who treated me and try to picture his name badge. Closing my eyes and turning up the temperature of the water, I let it hit the back of my neck like a massage. It's enough to set me off. My bad hand rests on the wall opposite and the other between my legs.

Afterwards, I wrap myself in a towel and catch sight of something in the mirror, a pattern of light on the skin of my collarbone, a shiny texture rippling in the reflection. A trick of the eye; perhaps the medication they gave me, maybe I'm having a reaction to it.

I'm due another dose.

It's almost lunchtime but I've barely any food in. So it's cereal at the window seat in the kitchen. This view isn't as good as the one from the beach. It faces inland and onto a street opposite a grocery. I watch people come and go. Single and able-bodied people. The children at home or safely stowed at school. The infirm stuck behind closed doors. Too risky.

It has rained and the puddles sit quietly, people swerve to avoid stepping in them. I'll have to go out for supplies. I dress and call at Vera's, to see if she needs anything. When she opens the door, she takes a noticeable step back from me, asks me how I'm feeling. I thank her for the soup that is still in my fridge.

"Should you be out?" she asks and I have to explain, again, that I don't have anyone to do this stuff for me. It's only across the road, anyway. She says she doesn't need anything, but I decide to see if they have any flowers. I'll leave them on her doorstep. As I slip away down the stairwell, I sense her staring after me and then my phone goes off. Work.

"Just checking in, Missy, how's the finger? You all tucked up in bed?"

"Boss. I'm okay, just nipping out for some bread."

"The place across from yours?"

"Yep."

"Okay, straight back and straight back to bed. Anything else to report?"

I think of the weird effect I saw on my collarbone. "No, just bored."

"I know, catch up on some sleep. Email some loved ones."

I laugh and end the call, looking for a basket outside of the grocer.

"Here, I've finished with mine," a voice from beside me. It's the medic.

"Oh, thank you!"

He is still in his scrubs, and holds a large bag of shopping across his chest. He tilts his head to one side and recognition drips over his face. "It's the dog bite patient."

"Yes... Hi."

"How is the injury?"

This time I read his badge, Marcus. Marcus the Medic.

"It's okay. It throbs a lot."

"You might need your dressings changed."

"Yes, I guess so."

"Come by the centre tomorrow. Ask for me."

"Okay... I will."

I get some supplies and some flowers for Vera and the owner gets his daughter to help me across and up to my flat.

"You can manage from here?" she says outside my door.

"Yes, thank you."

"You should get some rest, you look tired."

"That's the plan. Thank you"

I put the shopping away and heat Vera's soup. My energy gone, I eat it in bed.

The water is all around. My face is wet and cold from a breeze. I thrash around trying to find my footing but underneath are the depths. I try to tread water, try to keep my head above, but I'm so weak, I've nothing left to give. Ribbons of seaweed brush against my legs and tangle, each kick from me making it worse. I cry out with the only bit of energy left and wake myself up. My sheets are soaked with sweat and coiled around my hips and legs.

Dragging myself out of the bed, I pull off the clothes I fell asleep in and wander into the bathroom, passing the window in the moonlight. Something catches my eye. I adjust the slats of the blind. A large moth flutters at the streetlight outside and a mist hangs in the air. It has rolled in from the sea as it does most mornings. I sit and eat my breakfast, my eyes feeling like small holes that need lids. I'm so tired. Outside, the mist lifts and the supermarket opposite comes fully into view. The daughter is out there already, setting up the crates and unpacking deliveries.

I watch as the mist gets pushed along down the street by the breeze. I've never noticed before how solid it seems, craning my neck at the glass. Tumbling, floating down the street towards the junction that leads to the beach. It must be a trick of the morning, not yet light, it looks like the mist is forming a shape like a figure with arms outstretched. It hangs there and turns, the hollow place where the face should be, lifts and seems to look straight up at my window. Instinctively, I shrink back, feeling like I shouldn't be seeing whatever this is. I glance back directly opposite to the supermarket. The girl is still there but frozen, like a statue. I look back at the thing and it's hanging in the air like it's waiting for me. My finger throbs and still the mist hangs in that shape and I am transfixed by what it could be.

Within seconds, the sun reaches higher in the sky and the mist dissolves into nothing. Normal behaviour. I take a breath, realising I've been holding it. I must be seeing things. Opposite, there are customers queuing outside the supermarket, waiting for it to open. Things are ordinary again and I decide to get my dressing changed today first thing, promising myself I'll go back to bed on my return.

At the health centre, I'm thankful I'm only the second person there. Marcus sees me and calls me in.

"What's with the sunglasses? I barely recognised you." He gestures to a chair, and I sit.

"Oh, I'm not sleeping well and it's bright this morning, don't you think?"

"I hadn't noticed. I have to say this points to signs of infection; the aversion to light, the lack of sleep. Let's have a look then."

He washes his hands and peels off my bandages, and I stare at my finger. It's swollen with pus and there's a smell coming from it. The air stings.

"It's okay, we can sort this," he says. "We need to lance this now to stop it from spreading into your hand and causing more problems."

I take off my sunglasses and wipe my brow with my sleeve, suddenly hot.

"Your eyes," he says, looking from my finger to my face. "They are crammed with sleep."

I go to rub them, and he stops me.

"No, let me. I'll swab it too and send it to the lab. We need to make sure this is part of the eyes' normal function and not part of something bigger."

He cleans my eyes after taking a swab from each. They still feel small, swollen, like I can't see the same amount as I used to. I decide not to tell him this and wait and see what the lab results say. Let him focus on my finger.

"Right, let's sort this. I'm going to make one or two punctures into your finger. Avoiding the stitches if we can; they must feel tight under all this fluid."

I nod, unable to do much more. He uses a thick needle to make a hole close to the palm of my hand. I barely feel it. Yellow erupts, and he makes another opening just above the knuckle line. Again, it is like a dam being removed, but I barely feel it.

"Would you like to squeeze, or are you comfortable with me doing it? We need to remove all of it."

"Please continue, you're the expert."

He pushes on my finger and the pus spills from both places.

"I can feel it now, it's hurting."

"The pus acts like insulation, growing and throbbing against the bandages, but hiding its actual activity. A small amount of pus is okay, but this much can affect the blood and carry an infection around the body."

He doesn't flinch when I wince and cry out a few times. Afterwards, my finger feels like it's been in a fire and I head home with more medicine. For fighting any infection, he tells me. At my front door, I notice the flowers for Vera are still there. I was in such a daze this morning I hadn't spotted them. She mustn't have opened her door since I last saw her.

I strip the bed, my first and possibly only job other than getting better. With no energy to put on fresh bedding, I allow myself not to feel guilty and just sling it in the wash basket. Rest, just rest, just do normal things, he said, like have a bath. So I turn on the tap and add some bath salts Marcus gave me. I'm to use half a bag in one bath then shower normally between and in a week use the other half. By then I should be better. I swallow one of the new tablets.

As the bath runs, I remember the shard he'd pulled from my finger and find it stuck to the fridge in an envelope. Tipping it out onto the windowsill, there is a texture to it that would suggest a shell, and the shape is triangular, but on one edge is a serration that says one thing: Teeth. I remember trying to fling the thing off my finger. What could bite like that, and yet be so small, and live in the ocean or in the rock pools left behind by the tide?

Something had changed after the spillage, the reason for my job, the reason older and infirm folk were prisoners in

their homes, the reason for the curfew. It was more than just
a chemical spillage. It had changed things in the town.
Following that train of thought, it wouldn't be far-fetched
to discover a new species. But evolution doesn't work that
fast. I know that much. It was one year ago. I remember
sirens going off, rolling out of someone's bed, another
faceless fuck. There's none of that anymore. Marcus is the
first man I've seen that I've been attracted to and I'm unsure
if that's because my standards are different now, not that
they were ever high But it made me reassess. I didn't want
just anyone anymore. I want to merge.

Rain drops fall heavy on the window and I put the tooth
away and back on the fridge. I'll have to search online for
any place that might identify it. Thunder rolls outside, and
the sky grows dark. I light a few candles then slip into the
bath, plastic bag around my hand again. A drowsy feeling
washes over me and I lean back, resting my head on a
flannel and watching the rivulets of rain catch each other as
they run down the small window.

I'm dreaming, but not like before. I'm above my body,
asleep in the bath. The candles have burnt right down and
the room is near dark. The rain has stopped and there are no

other sounds, not even my own breath. I know it's a dream but I cannot wake just yet, I'm so tired. I edge closer to me in the tub and can see something crusted again in my eyes. I'm sitting on the floor next to me asleep in the bath, the tablets must cause this, what a trip. Then I notice my face, the real me in the water, my face is coming loose, drifting on the surface of the water. I look down at the rest of me and parts of my skin are loosening or even floating on the surface of the bath. Underneath in the water, I can't see my limbs or my body. It's like they have dissolved and left the skin behind. My mouth fills with water as I shake myself in the bath.

"Wake up, wake up!"

I sit bolt upright in the water. The candles are still lit; the rain is still hammering at the window. Shaking the dream from my head, I splash my eyes and remove the crud, then climb out, and head straight for bed.

There is someone banging on my door. It's morning, I can see the glow of the sun through my eyelids. They are stuck together again. It hurts to open them. The people at the door are banging and shouting.

"Give me a minute," I shout back, voice grating my throat as I force it out of me. I grope around for my dressing gown in the bed and pull it on. Rubbing at my eyes, they feel gritty again, but something is off. I can pick off the sleep crusts, but my eyelids seem sealed. A panic rises in my chest like a rabid weasel. They are still at the door. Fuck, what do I do?

"Coming!"

I stand and feel my way to the bedroom door then into the hallway, siding along with my wall. I know this flat, every inch. Fuck, my eyes. I can't let them in.

"What is the problem?"

"Can you open the door, please?"

"I'm unwell. On bed rest. Been told to isolate. I can't see anyone," I say, leaning on the door. There's a chance that they could force their way in. If there's an outbreak, they'll be all geared up for it.

"It's your neighbour, across the hall here. When was the last time you saw her?" The man's mouth must be inches away from my ear. Through the door, I can hear him breathing and his radio crackling in the background.

"Vera? Yes, I saw her maybe two or three days ago. She brought over some soup as I've been sick."

"You are sick and you let her in?" The tone was accusatory.

"No, no! We spoke through the door like this. She left the soup on my doormat." I lied. "What has happened to her?"

"She's dead. Her son had to break down the door. You are probably the last person she spoke to."

I slide down the door until I'm sat on the floor and fiddle with the dressing at my finger. It is finally feeling better.

"Are you okay? Did you leave these flowers outside Vera's door?"

"Yes. I did." Have I killed Vera? I slip the bandages from my hand.

"Can you slide your ID under the door, please? For our report."

"Can I ask what happened to her?" I remove the splint and flex the finger.

"We can't release any information until we've gathered all the data."

"I'll have to dig it out. Can you give me some time?" The eye at the end of my finger blinks open. I can see again. It's like looking through binoculars. I hear him step away from my door and call his supervisor on the radio.

"Wow." The panic I felt earlier subsides. It's replaced by something else.

"What was that, Miss? Are you okay in there?"

"What? Sorry, yes, I'm fine. I think I can find it now if you want to hold on." I know exactly where my ID is, in the uniform I was wearing on the night of the incident. Standing, more confidently this time with my weird new viewpoint, I move back through to my bedroom. My eye sees it immediately and I'm awkward as I unfasten it from the front of the jacket, not wanting to poke or damage my new eye.

I slide it under my front door to the man outside.

"Ah, you're one of us. Sorry to bother you, Miss Eldon."

"No problem."

He slides it back. "Get well soon." He retreats from the door. I take a breath.

This new perspective is strange. Everything feels too big. My surroundings suddenly don't feel like home anymore. The darkness around my peripheral vision seems to throb and reach for me. There's no fresh air. I'm trapped here. Perhaps another bath will help, give me a chance to figure out what to do.

The bath fills, and a craving for crisps overwhelms me. In the kitchen, I find an opened bag of pretzels. Stale, but the salt crystals send sublime messages to my brain. I'm thankful my mouth is still normal, even if my eyes aren't. I'm careful not to get crumbs in my new eye. Suddenly know how to feel better.

I get as much as I can from the kitchen, dishwasher salt, table salt, sea salt, even the pink stuff that a friend bought me and I've never used. Then empty them all into my bath, along with the rest of the salt the medic gave me. I add some cold and let it run, desperate to get in quickly.

I strip and feel it immediately on stepping in; Home. My eye clocks the level of the water, it's at the overflow. I remove the cover, sit down, lean back and dissolve, slipping away back to sea.

Book Club Discussion

1. What was your favourite story in the book?

2. What was your least favourite?

3. Did any of the stories remind you of a different story (*a different book or movie*)? What did it remind you of and why?

4. Who is this collection for? Who should read it?

5. How were the supernatural or horror elements of the stories used? Were they metaphors for something else? Why or why not?

6. How did it impact you? Do you think you'll remember it in a few months or years?

7. Did any of the stories book spook you, or get under your skin, in any way?

8. Did you want more from any of the stories? For example, more about the characters, or a longer story?

9. If you could ask the author one question about this collection, what would it be?

10. What three words would you use to best describe this book.

BONUS STORY

Sign up to Susan's mailing list to get an extra short story.

> *A woman travels to Rome to work on an*
> *archaeological dig. An Ancient has been woken*
> *and is ready for revenge.*

> *This is feminist cosmic horror.*

Go to **https://BookHip.com/RTTDHA**

About the Author

Susan Earlam lives on the edges of the Peak District in Cheshire, England, with her husband, two daughters, and Billy the cat.

Since 2010, she has written for a variety of media outlets, but the call of the strange and unusual grew irresistible. Now she mixes words like potions at her desk.

She procrastinates by writing shorter, and weirder, stuff. Her first novel, Earthly Bodies, was published in April 2021.

susanearlam.com

Twitter and Instagram @SusanEarlam

SOURCES

The following gives the first publication details of each story, where relevant.

- "Baby" first published by *Reflex Fiction,* October 2019.

- "Feathers" first published by *Greenhouse Books,* November 2019.

- "Exuvia" first published and collected in *Strange Abrasions by Comma Press,* October 2021.

- "Queen of the Underworld" first published in *The Debutante journal.* Issue two, 2020.

- "The Treatment" first published in *Cabinet of Heed* Issue 33, May 2020.

- "The Carer" first published in *The Debutante journal.* Issue one, 2019.

- "Milk" first published by *Reflex Fiction*, October 2020.

ACKNOWLEDGEMENTS

It takes a lot to write a book, especially in a pandemic. And hell, this isn't even a full-on beast of a novel. But these short stories helped me get through some hard times.

Thanks to, Comma Press and Andy Murray for facilitating and hosting the horror course, from which some of these tales were born. To the cohort on that course for being the tribe of horror pals to push me that bit deeper into the genre and beyond.

To my Flash Fiction group, thanks for reading, your feedback, and for showing up every month when it seemed the world outside was falling apart. Thanks to my editor, Elle, for the nuanced suggestions. Thanks to my first readers for their generosity and time. Thanks to Ana Milani for the beautiful illustration and front cover.

To my husband and daughters, thank you for your support and for bringing me back to myself, time and time again. Thanks to Billy the cat for trying to teach me about rest. To my friends, in real life and beyond, thank you for being my cheerleading squad. Knowing you are reading my words makes me happy.

Bonus content ~ First Chapter of Earthly Bodies - Year 2058

Rebecca, June

This will be the last time we see each other. Not because I'm going to try again, but because I've received the answer I hoped for. Yes, I'm leaving Earth.

"Would you look at the camera, sis? Have you changed your hair? Your hair looks lighter, different. It's been ages."

Sam is snapping away, testing the light. The plant I bought him is perched on the windowsill next to me. Will he care for it after I'm gone? I squirm; not wanting my photo taken, sat here on the floor of his small studio. I've been doing the rounds all morning, visiting a handful of people here in Scredda. Leaving him until last. Kaolin Heights used to be an affluent neighbourhood, not anymore and I feel scruffy, wearing my oldest pair of black jeans and a sleeveless tee. I'm scared that if I look at the camera, he'll be able to read my thoughts, see the secret in my eyes.

Sam moves around, taking photos, not really expecting an answer. He enjoys life here, I'm sure he will be okay. I will miss his innocent way of looking at the world, but I must think of myself now. Being here isn't good for me. I need a fresh start."Do you have your old Instant here?" I finally say, shaking off my thoughts. "Let's get a shot of us together for a change."He digs through a couple of cardboard boxes until he finds it."There's one shot left.""Well it's fate then, isn't it? A fair exchange: a plant for a picture." Grabbing his arm, I pull him down next to me, his beard brushes the side of my face.

C-CLICK

I catch the photo out of the top of the camera before he even has a chance to try. He pulls that face, the same one he did when we were kids, when I'd won.

"Hey, let me see!"

"Sorry, Sam, I didn't realise the time. I've got to go." I hold the photo to my chest.

If I stay any longer, I'll end up telling him everything. I can't even look at him. Swallowing the tears in my throat, I jump up from the floor and say my goodbyes—leaving my bewildered brother at the door.

He'll receive a letter once I'm gone. I've made sure to follow the instructions exactly.

It's dusk as I head out onto the street and finally look at the photograph. Sam is right. My hair does look lighter, but my skin is still near-translucent, partly covered by stories etched on with the tattooist's needle. I look like a fairy goth and Sam, my sweet, sweet brother, looks like Dad.

The tears come freely, and I start to run. The once pretty streets are crumbling. The pavements are full of cracks, the roads are full of potholes. Buildings sit derelict but for the homeless, and someone tries to sell me drugs as I run past. I weave in and out of zombie-like users. Many places are like this now, not just here. People have lost more than hope.

~

Back at my flat and out of the muggy air. I stand for a minute and catch my breath. It doesn't feel like home. I've sold or given everything away, even my bed. The rucksack is waiting for me by the door. Packing was easy, once I'd begun to purge stuff, carefully taking only a few favourite pieces of clothing. I saved the most space for personal items. These are classed as Earth memorabilia in the travel instructions. The bag sits there, waiting to exhale its belongings into a new life; my new life.

I have a few hours to kill before I need to leave. Everything feels shadowy and underhand, done in darkness. I know this is because of the secrecy, but I hate to lie.

My mouth is dry, but there's nothing to drink. I had the water switched off, so I could settle my bills. I test the tap in the small kitchen anyway, and a dribble comes out, which I slurp at like a cat.

As instructed, the warm travelling clothes are folded by the side of my rucksack. Sitting on top is the wristband I must wear from now on, it's preloaded with my journey details so I won't get any awkward questions when I'm scanned at the travel gates. I strap it to my wrist and commit myself fully. Then I slip the clothes on, their heat makes me drowsy. The jumper was my husband's. Its itchy fibres tickle my skin. Lying on my side, I draw the bag under my head and pull my arms in close to my face, and I caress my cheeks with wool-encompassed fingers gripping the jumper. It makes me feel like he's here, the sensation of him fills me up, and I can forget he is gone.

~

Space tourists are common now. I'm on an electric coach, it has small, long windows which remind me of letterboxes. The people here will have saved up for their trips around Earth, or even to one of the Lunar Orbital Space Stations. My ticket is one way. We pull to a stop and almost everyone gets off. We must be on the borders of Wales; I've read there is a launch site here. I've been told only to exit when prompted by a facilitator, a MAGIE, who will make sure my transfer goes smoothly. The MAGIE are robotic humanoids. A type of Artificial Intelligence: Mindful, Able, Genderless, Inter-operable Entities. Pitched as useful, they are a way of keeping watch over citizens, like spies. I try to avoid them. Whoever is left on the coach at the end of this leg, will be coming with me, further north of here to somewhere near the Shetlands. A couple of people get on—they don't seem to know each other—and we pull away. There are around twelve people who must have boarded while I've been dozing. I'm relieved to see that it's mostly women. All the same, I keep my eyes low, not ready for small talk. Out of the window, I catch the eye of a teenage boy that has just been dropped off on to the grey tarmac, he leans back on

the railings, the epitome of teenage disinterest. His parents
are obviously rich; they look antiseptic. His mum busies
herself with her MAGIEpad while the dad takes multiple
puffs of an inhaler. The boy stares at me with an accusing
curiosity, looking out from the grey. I feel sad. Sad for what
could have been. Sad that his parents are the way they are,
and sad because all life has potential, unless you aren't on
the list. What will happen to these people left behind? The
fact is, I wouldn't be on this coach if we'd had a child. 'One
extreme always leads to another,' Mum would always say as
she sat crying in front of the news. It's been that way for as
long as I remember. Despite three applications, we'd never
been given the go ahead. Christian had blamed himself.
Even if we had received a parenting license, there was no
guarantee of a full-term pregnancy, and medical
intervention was only for the rich.

I settle down for another attempt at napping, rolling my
coat up and plugging it between my shoulder and head. I
lean against the window, quickly realising I haven't worn
this coat since last winter. It's matted with dog hair;
Juniper's. My parents' dog that had come to live with me
when she got too much for Dad.

We pass what must be acres of scrap metal yards. Far into
the smog I can see cars, boats, even a few helicopters at
different stages of corrosion, stacked in wonky columns. I
drift into a fitful sleep. The domes of my old workplace
blend with visions of grey, rocky cliffs and spikey,
foreboding trees which beckon at me from the gloom.

~

Spending my days inside the Eden Project had been a dream come true. A man-made botanical paradise and the blueprint for many other eco-dome projects around the world. I'd felt at home there, recreating how Earth used to be by working as a storyteller. My job was to capture the imagination of visitors and transport them into different worlds, times, and places. I was good at it and believe it's part of the reason I'm on this elopement. It had been a sad, slow decline for the park. The funding began to dry up first, some of the staff were let go. Then the park couldn't be maintained at its usual standard and, as word got out, fewer visitors came through the gates.

Eventually it became the focus of a guerrilla group. They managed to infiltrate the networks of the remaining staff at the park, playing on their insecurities about the future. They'd used the lush environment to grow and manufacture illegal drugs—a highly addictive cannabis hybrid. In the end, I didn't know who to trust; friends had turned against one another.

Before the park's downward spiral, I'd got one of my first pieces of body art—depicting the biodomes and the lush greenery hinted at inside. It sits on my left thigh, reminding me of a beautiful and idyllic time of my life. I met Christian around that time, too.

"Wakey, wakey." Somebody nudges me in the arm. My thoughts fade instantly. There must have been another stop after I'd nodded off. I hadn't felt anyone sit down. "Looks like we have to get off," they say as a hooded figure passes us down the aisle of the coach. I roll my shoulders up to my ears and push out my rib cage, stretching my spine. Here and now is where I need to focus, not the past—especially when looking at it with a rosy perspective. I grab my backpack from the cage above my head. Everyone else has left already and are standing outside, waiting. I'm the last one. For the briefest moment, I contemplate hiding under the seats or at the back of the storage cages: a stowaway ready to be taken back, not wanting to face whatever unknowns are beyond this point. The thought passes, and I quickly slip down the aisle to join the others.

~

This is it. I've arrived at the place where my future begins. The sun is setting, I can see it here, the sky is so clear, so big. A battered Saxa Vord Resort sign looks down at us at the side of the track. We are at the very north of the Shetland Isles, roads as I know them don't exist here. There are patches of small shrubs and heather making headway among the abandoned low breezeblock huts we've been dropped beside. It feels bleak but is much leafier here than I anticipated. The shades of browns and greens bring back flashes of my work in Cornwall and the past I'm leaving behind.

There are around twenty in the group. We aren't the first to be deposited here. It's been made clear in the documentation that there are other groups, feeling ready for a different future, trying to prepare for the unknown. We are in an open area, with a slope to one side. I hear the sea, a new companion on this last leg. In the distance I can see some basic cabins and a small group of figures coming towards us. The group quietens and a palpable sense of foreboding spreads among us. The sense of isolation here— at the crossing to another world—is frighteningly real.

"We are in the middle of nowhere for sure," someone says. I can almost see the eye roll, despite the voice coming from behind me.

"What have I done?" someone else begins, sinking to the floor, unable to process the remote situation. Other murmurs start from the small crowd, but having not spoken to anyone on the trip up here, I don't want to start now. It begins to rain, a misty drizzle that hangs in the air making everything damp, leaving a coat of droplets wherever it falls. I feel like I'm being covered in dew. I tilt my face up to the sky to really feel it on my skin. The sky is heavy with more moisture, perhaps even snow? The weather is harder to predict than ever these days, a tempestuous child: the product of our systemic abuse.

The figures coming towards us are clearer now. There is a tall woman in the centre, with strawberry blonde hair tied back in a ponytail and an open friendly face. The woman is in step with two MAGIE, and my stomach flips. More MAGIE, I should've known the one on the coach wouldn't be the only one for a project like this. Of course, it makes sense that there would be a MAGIE presence. I have no choice but to interact with them—it's a means to an end. The woman in the middle is wearing wellies and a long, thick coat. Her hands are in her pockets. We can all see plainly that she is talking to the MAGIE. The trio get within earshot and the woman stops talking. The path they are on is more like a track, well-worn and narrow. The MAGIE flanking the woman break free from their formation and move to circle us. My experience with MAGIE has been mixed, mostly occurring through the education system. The lab technicians and administration staff at my school used a couple of MAGIE. They performed their duties well enough but never integrated with the school population. I'd always felt that they were there to collate and report, more than anything else.The group here seems to feel the same way. A whisper of apprehension, hands clutching backpacks a little tighter, making knuckles white.

The MAGIE are checking to see who is here. The strawberry blonde-haired woman positions herself close to us newcomers."Welcome, welcome." She has a calm voice, but there is a faint shrill to it that she struggles to hide. "We are glad you made the choice to attend this retreat. We hope at its conclusion you will all be able to go further onwards. That is down to you and what you can bring us, what you are willing to share and perhaps even unlearn. My name is Doctor Annabel Morin, and I'll be your main point of contact here at Saxa Vord." The doctor was looking at each of us in turn, attempting to make eye contact with everyone. I want to hold her eye, but instead I look slightly past her, over her shoulder, annoying myself."You should all know by now that there will be weeks of intense coaching and counselling here. Hypnosis, dream therapy, and more. We need to ensure you will hold up when the departure time comes. I'm assuming there are no immediate questions?"

Questions? We all have questions.

"I know you'll all be very tired and want to freshen up, so let's head in."

Spinning on her rubber heel, Dr Morin heads back towards the buildings in the distance. I spot a man rushing to catch up with her. I'm tired, and lag behind, withdrawing to the edges of the group as we move towards the cabins. Looking down at my feet, I feel grateful to have steady land, real earth and not concrete, under my feet again.

"You must keep up with the group, Rebecca." A stern, robotic voice comes from over my shoulder. Why am I surprised the MAGIE knows my name? The sloping rooftops of the buildings appear to be at acute angles and run down, almost to the ground. We enter the biggest building, from a door on the wall-side. The interior is surprisingly rustic. I'd expected to walk into a clinical environment, but the heart of the Saxa Vord compound— where I'd assumed things would be shiny and new—instead feels warm, almost cosy. Through the large window at the other end of the room, I can see that the warren of small bungalows is connected by boardwalks. In here, there is a long communal dining table and a kitchen set up at that end of the space. This space is warmed by a fire, a real fire. There are blankets, musty sofas dotted around, and bookshelves on nearly every wall. I can feel myself smiling, and I'm growing a little overwhelmed and dizzy, but I also sense safety. I let the feelings wash over me, grateful to feel them. It's going to be okay. I hear myself let out a big sigh as

I sink down into the nearest chair. Dare I relax? Seems I can't help it. It feels idyllic. I want to drop my guard. It's exhausting being alert and suspicious all the time. The sleep I'd managed on the journey wasn't enough. I let it come for me here; my limbs heavy, my eyes close.